DEPENDABLE

DETERMINED

FAIR

LUCKY

OPTIMISTIC

ADVENTUROUS

For Daniel,
who grew up just right

Charise wants to give a Big thank you to the following
people for their photo contribution to this book:
Amy, Ruth, Daniel, Zia, David, Christopher, John,
Barbara, Carol, Dema, Jack, Nina and Brock.

Then also yippee for...

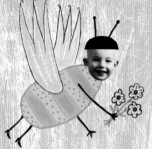

Jeremy's determination,
Victoria's optimism,
Kristen's imagination,
and Summer's patience.

Copyright © 2001 by Charise Mericle Harper.
All rights reserved.

Book design by Kristen M. Nobles.
Typeset in Providence.
The illustrations in this book were rendered in acrylic on masonite board.
Printed in Hong Kong.

ISBN 0-8118-2905-7

Library of Congress Cataloging-in-Publication Data available

Distributed in Canada by Raincoast Books
9050 Shaughnessy Street, Vancouver, British Columbia V6P 6E5

10 9 8 7 6 5 4 3 2 1

Chronicle Books LLC
85 Second Street, San Francisco, California 94105
www.chroniclebooks.com/Kids

When I Grow Up

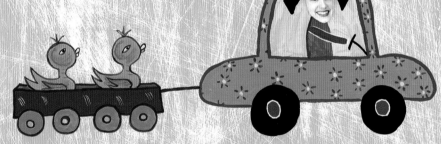

by Charise Mericle Harper

chronicle books · san francisco

When I
I wan

grow up

to be...

We'll run so fast the MONSTER
Won't even see us.

THOUGHTFUL

You can have ONE of my Mittens, I'll keep my hand in my Pocket.

We Look good enough to be ON T.V.

DETERMINED

I know we can do it even if it takes all DAY.

Let's make something out of this box.

DEPENDABLE

You can always count on me to (SAVE) you a Seat.

FAIR

8 Cookies for you,
8 Cookies for me
And 8 Cookies for you.

PATIENT

I can hardly wait until it's my turn to PULL.

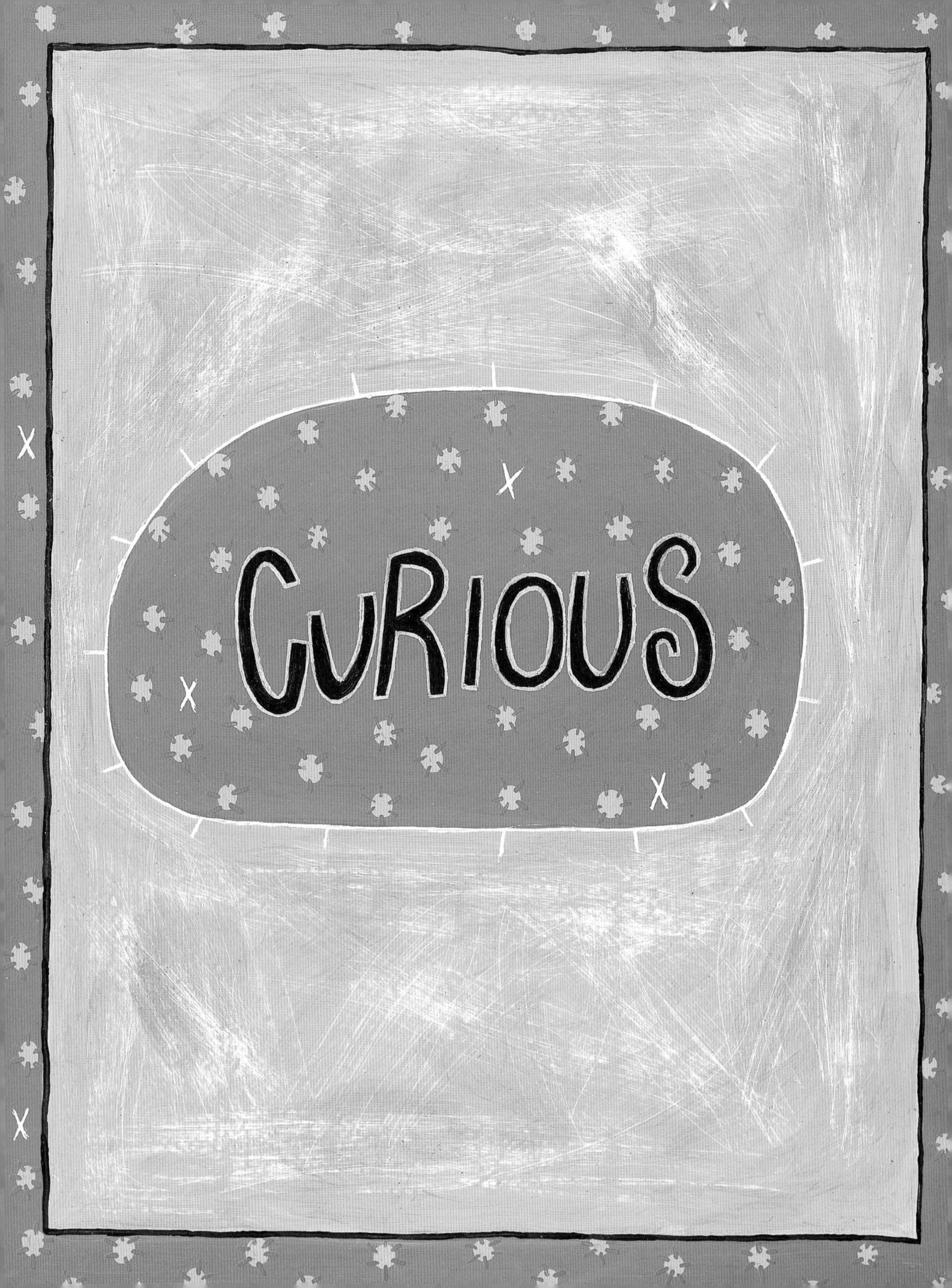
CURIOUS

Why Doesn't Everybody have the Same FAVORITE CoLoR?

Don't forget your SUNGLASSES.

FAIR

Today I

DEPENDABLE

CONFIDENT

LUCKY

ADVENTUROUS

THOUGHTFUL

BRAVE

will be...

DETERMINED

GENEROUS

UNDERSTANDING

OPTIMISTIC

CURIOUS

IMAGINATIVE

PATIENT

GENEROUS

CONFIDENT

CURIOUS

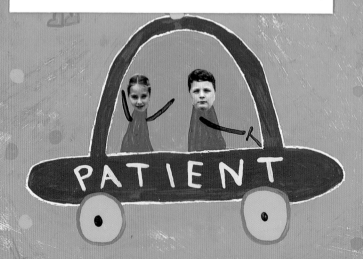

PATIENT